FOR LOVE OR MONEY

adapted by Wendy Wax   illustrated by Piero Piluso

based on the teleplay by Cynthia True

SCHOLASTIC INC.

New York Toronto London Auckland Sydney
Mexico City New Delhi Hong Kong Buenos Aires

Timmy Turner should have
been cleaning his room.
Instead he was listening to
his fairy godparents argue.
"Nag!" yelled Cosmo.
"I am not a nag!" shouted Wanda.

"What's that noise?"
called Mrs. Turner.
She opened the door.
"Timmy Turner!" she yelled.
"This place is a mess. Just wait
until your father gets home!"

"I am home!" said Mr. Turner.

"You are so pretty when
  you are angry," he told Mrs. Turner.

"And you are so handsome
  when you say I am pretty,"
  said Mrs. Turner.

They began to dance.

"Wow, did you see that?"

Timmy asked Cosmo and Wanda.

"When Dad got all mushy,

Mom forgot that she was angry!"

"Well, I am still angry," said Wanda.

"Let's dance, sweetie," said Cosmo.

"I would love to!" Wanda said.

"Wow!" said Timmy.

"Love really does make anger go away."

"Timmy, your mom and I cannot stop dancing!" said Mr. Turner. "Guess who is coming to watch you," Mrs. Turner called as they danced around the room.

Just then Vicky stormed
into the house.
"You have two choices," she said.
"Clean all the toilets in the house
or drink out of them."
"But I am not thirsty, and I am
not a dog!" Timmy cried.

"That's it!" Timmy said

to his fairy godparents.

"I wish Vicky had a boyfriend—

someone romantic to make her

forget to be mean."

POOF!

The doorbell rang.

Vicky opened the door.

"What do you want?" she snapped.

"I am Ricky, and you are cute,"

said a boy.

"Want to buy a magazine?"

"You stole those magazines
from the Turners' mailbox,"
said Vicky. "But you are handsome."
She flashed him a smile.

Timmy went to the door.

"Hey, what is going on?" he asked.

"Go to bed, twerp," said Vicky
and Ricky at the same time.

"It's working!" said Timmy.

"Vicky and Ricky are in love."

"I am taking your mother out,"
    said Mr. Turner. "Where is Vicky?"
"She is outside with her
    new boyfriend," said Timmy.
"Sweet!" said Mr. Turner.
"With two babysitters we can
    stay out twice as long!"

But having two babysitters
was no fun.
"I wish they would break up,"
said Timmy.
"Da Rules say we cannot break up
true love," Wanda reminded him.
"Only fake love."

"Maybe their love is fake,"
said Timmy.

"If it is, then we would have to
prove it," said Wanda.

Timmy and his godparents spied

on the lovebirds.

"Do you babysit a lot, cupcake?"

Ricky asked.

"I sure do, cookie," said Vicky.

"Then you must be rich!"

said Ricky.

"See?" whispered Timmy.

"Ricky does not really love Vicky.

He only likes her for her money."

"But she loves him," said Wanda.

"I will just have to break them

up myself," said Timmy.

"To the Internet!"

Timmy ran upstairs to his room
and turned on his computer.
"I will find Ricky a rich new
girlfriend," he said.

Wanda helped him post an ad
on the Internet. It said:
NICE, SWEET, SINGLE TEEN MALE
SEEKS GIRL WITH TONS OF MONEY.
"You have got mail!"
said the computer.

"Hey, Ricky!" called Timmy.

"Check this out!"

Ricky came in and read:

SINGLE TEEN BEAUTY

WANTS TO SHARE MILLIONS!

"Hi, handsome," said a voice
from the computer.
"I am Darcy. If you want to
be rich, click on **I DO**
and marry me."
Ricky clicked on **I DO**.

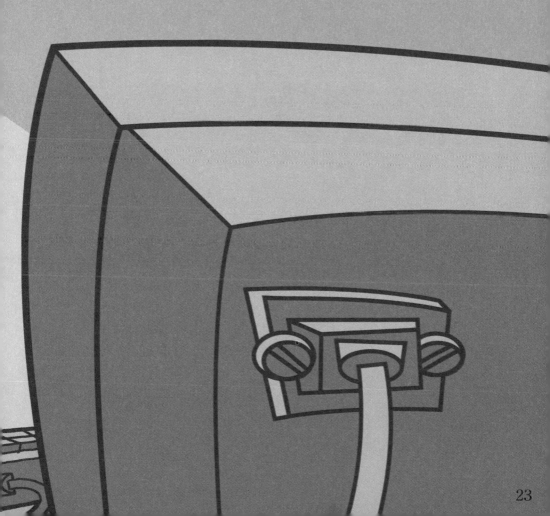

"I now pronounce you
man and wife," said the computer.

"I am rich!" shouted Ricky.

"Hey, what about Vicky?"
asked Timmy.

"Who?" asked Ricky.

"Your girlfriend," said Timmy.

"Oh, yeah," said Ricky, getting up.

"I can't wait to tell her the news."

Ricky hurried downstairs.

"I missed you, sweetie," said Vicky.

"And I miss my rich new wife
who I just married," said Ricky,
and he left.
Vicky stood at the door crying.

"I want my money!" Ricky called
   when he got to Darcy's house.

"And I want my first married kiss,"
   Darcy said.

"No way! You are Mr. Crocker's
   mother!" said Ricky.

"But at least you are rich."

"Not anymore," said Mr. Crocker.

"Mommy spent all of her money
   years ago, Stepdad!"

Meanwhile, things were back
to normal at the Turner house.
"Wow, Timmy!" said Wanda.
"You really broke them up."
Suddenly, they heard banging
in the next room.

"And now Vicky is madder than ever," said Cosmo.

"Where are you, twerp!" yelled Vicky.

"Don't just sit there, Timmy," said Cosmo. "Run!"

The Turners came home feeling happy.
Then Mrs. Turner saw Timmy's room.
"Timmy Turner!" she yelled.
"Clean your room now or you will be
grounded for life!"